MARVEL UNIVERSE ULTIMATE SPIDER-MAN & THE AVENGERS. Contains material originally published in magazine form as MARVEL UNIVERSE ULTIMATE SPIDER-MAN #29-31 and MARVEL UNIVERSE AVENGERS ASSEMBLE #13. First printing 2016. ISBN# 978-0-7851-9578-8. Published by MARVEL WORLDWIDE, INC., a subsidiary of MARVEL ENTERTAINMENT, LLC. OFFICE OF PUBLICATION: 135 West 50th Street, New York, NY 10020.

Printed in the U.S.A. ALAN FINE, President, Marvel Entertainment; DAN BUCKLEY, President, TV, Publishing and Brand Management; JOE QUESADA, Chief Creative Officer; TOM BREVOORT, SVP of Publishing; DAVID BOGART, SVP of Operations & Procurement, Publishing; C.B. CEBULSKI, VP of International Development & Brand Management; DAVID GABRIEL, SVP Print, Sales & Marketing; JIM O'KEEFE, VP of Operations & Logistics; DAN CARR, Executive Director of Publishing Technology; SUSAN CRESPI, Editorial Operations Manager; ALEX MORALES, Publishing Operations Manager; STAN LEE, Chairman Emeritus. For information regarding advertising in Marvel Comics or on Marvel.com, please contact Jonathan Rheingold, VP of Custom Solutions & Ad Sales, at jrheingold@marvel.com. For Marvel subscription inquiries, please call 800-217-9158. **Manufactured between 11/13/2015 and 12/21/2015 by SHERIDAN BOOKS, INC., CHELSEA, MI, USA.**

10 9 8 7 6 5 4 3 2 1

MARVEL ULTIMATE SPIDER-MAN

AVENGERS ASSEMBLE

BASED ON THE TV SERIES WRITTEN BY
MAN OF ACTION, EUGENE SON, JOE FALLON, FRANK TIERI, KEVIN BURKE & CHRIS "DOC" WYATT

DIRECTED BY
PHIL PIGNOTTI, ALEX SOTO & JEFF ALLEN

ADAPTED BY
JOE CARAMAGNA

EDITOR
SEBASTIAN GIRNER

CONSULTING EDITORS
MARK BASSO & JON MOISAN

SENIOR EDITOR
MARK PANICCIA

SPIDER-MAN CREATED BY STAN LEE & STEVE DITKO

AVENGERS CREATED BY STAN LEE & JACK KIRBY

Collection Editor: **Alex Starbuck**
Assistant Editor: **Sarah Brunstad**
Editors, Special Projects: **Jennifer Grünwald & Mark D. Beazley**
Senior Editor, Special Projects: **Jeff Youngquist**
SVP Print, Sales & Marketing: **David Gabriel**
Book Designer: **Adam Del Re**

Editor In Chief: **Axel Alonso**
Chief Creative Officer: **Joe Quesada**
Publisher: **Dan Buckley**
Executive Producer: **Alan Fine**

SPECIAL THANKS TO MARVEL ANIMATION, PRODUCT FACTORY, JUDY STEPHENS & ARUNE SINGH

Based on "Run Pig Run"

GRRR!
KNOCK IT OFF!
I KNOW YOU'RE HUNGRY, STOMACH, BUT I HAD NO TIME FOR AUNT MAY'S WHEAT-CAKES THIS MORNING.
TODAY'S PICTURE DAY! AND FOR ONCE IN MY LIFE...
...I WANT TO GET IT RIGHT.
YOU'RE JUST GONNA HAVE TO WAIT FOR LUNCH.
YO, SPIDEY!
YOU HUNGRY?
HOW'S ABOUT SOME BREAKFAST? IT'S ON THE HOUSE!
HMM...MY SPIDER-SENSE IS TINGLING, BUT IT ALWAYS DOES THAT AROUND STREET FOOD.
OH, WELL. YOU KNOW WHAT THEY SAY:
BREAKFAST IS THE MOST IMPORTANT MEAL OF THE DAY. CHOMP!
HA HA HA HA!

VTT!
HOW IS YOUR HOT DOG, SPIDER-MAN?
LOKI?!
WHAT DO YOU WANT?
WAIT, DID YOU SPIT IN MY FOOD?
NOT EVEN I AM THAT MERCILESS.
THE HOT DOG WAS ENCHANTED.
POOF!
GIVING A LITERAL MEANING TO THE PHRASE "YOU ARE WHAT YOU EAT."
WHREEEET!
YOU MEAN I'M A P-P-P-P-P-PIG?!

CONSIDER IT A PLAYFUL RIPOSTE TO OUR LAST ENCOUNTER WHEN YOU INTERFERED WITH MY PLANS OF CONQUEST.
I'M SIMPLY RETURNING THE FAVOR.
YOU THINK THIS WILL STOP ME?
CHANGE ME BACK BEFORE I--
BRRRROOOOOOOOOOOOO--
WHAT WAS THAT?
THAT WAS YOUR CUE TO RUN.
HUZZAH!
THERE IS OUR TARGET! LET THE HUNT BEGIN!
H-HUNT?

PANT
PANT
PANT
PANT
SNORT
FT!
FT!
FT!
FT!
FT!
FT!
FT!
FT!
FT!
FT!
SLAY THE SWINE!
SHUNK!
LOOK, FELLAS, I'M NOT REALLY A--
A TALKING PIG?
EVEN BETTER!
I'LL HANG ITS HEAD OVER MY FIREPLACE NEXT TO THE OTHERS!
OTHERS?!
WHOOOSH!

KLANG!
GAHH--
HEY--WHY AM I NOT SLICED INTO HAM STEAKS RIGHT NOW?
WHOOSH!
THOR!

THANKS! YOU REALLY SAVED MY CURLY LI'L TAIL.
SPIDER-MAN? A BOAR?!
LET ME GUESS--MY BROTHER LOKI HAD A HAND IN THIS.
YOU HAVE NO BUSINESS HERE, SON OF ODIN. I SAW HIM FIRST!
WHAT IS HE TALKING ABOUT?
IT IS THE DAY OF ASGARD'S WILD HUNT.
ONCE A YEAR MY WORLD'S FINEST HUNTERS RIDE OFF TO SKEWER A PRIZE BOAR TO BE EATEN AT A GRAND FEAST IN VALHALLA AT SUNDOWN.
IT APPEARS THAT YOU ARE THIS YEAR'S PREY.
ME?! THOR, YOU HAVE TO DO SOMETHING!
AS A MEMBER OF THE ROYAL FAMILY, HE CAN'T STOP US WITHOUT GOING AGAINST HIS OWN FATHER'S LAWS.
AYE. I'M AFRAID THE EXECUTIONER IS CORRECT. I CAN NOT STOP THIS HUNT.
BUT I CAN SLOW THEM DOWN!
KRAKA-BOOM!

JUST TELL THEM I'M NOT A PIG!
THAT WILL NOT WORK.
QUICKLY! TAKE HOLD OF MY HAMMER MJOLNIR!
WHY WOULD I DO--
--THAAAAAAAAAAAAAAAA
AAAAAAAAAAAAAAA
KLUNG!
LUCKILY, I LANDED RIGHT IN FRONT OF MIDTOWN HIGH! AT LEAST I KNOW I HAVE REAL FRIENDS HERE THAT I CAN COUNT ON.
HA! HA!
HA! HA! HA!
HA!
HA!
HA!
HA!

AW, COME ON! THIS IS SERIOUS! YOU GUYS ARE SUPPOSED TO BE MY FRIENDS!
THERE IT IS!
YOU CAN'T HIDE FROM US, SWINE! OUR WOLVES HAVE YOUR SCENT!
WHOA. THIS IS SERIOUS.
SEE?! GO DO A WARDROBE CHANGE. I'LL KEEP THEM OCCUPIED.
LOOK! I AM NOT A PIG, OKAY?! THIS IS ALL A MISUNDERSTANDING!
AYE...
...THAT IS JUST WHAT A TALKING PIG WOULD SAY!
SQUEEEEEEE!
SHUNK! SHUNK! SHUNK!
YOINK!
HEADS UP, SPIDER-HAM!

I GOT YOU!
DID YOU JUST CALL ME SPIDER-HAM?
I CAN CALL YOU ANYTHING I WANT. I JUST SAVED YOUR BACON!
GROAN.
AFTER HIM!
WHO'S UP FOR TOSSING THE OL' PIGSKIN?
NOVA, DON'T--
THANKS!
THUMP!
NICE CATCH, POWER MAN!
KROOM!
THERE YOU ARE!

I'VE NEVER SEEN SUCH FIGHT IN A PIG BEFORE. YOU MUST BE ESPECIALLY DELICIOUS!
IRON FIST, GO LONG!
THIS IS HUMILIATING!
WHOOOSH!
GOT HIM!
THUMP!
GUYS, THIS WAY!
SHUNK!
WE'RE RIGHT BEHIND YOU, WHITE TIGER!

MEANWHILE...
I NEEDED YOUR HELP.
SO YOU BROUGHT THE FIGHT HERE? TO MY SCHOOL?
IF THERE IS ANYONE WHO CAN AID OUR FRIEND, IT IS YOU, SON OF COUL.
YOU HAVE A POINT. NOT ONLY AM I PHIL COULSON, HIGH SCHOOL PRINCIPAL...
PRINCIPAL
VMM!
VMM!
VMM!
...I'M ALSO AN AGENT OF S.H.I.E.L.D.!
"I CAN HANDLE ANYTHING!"
ARE THEY GONE?
HARDLY, YOUNGLINGS!

THERE'S NOWHERE LEFT TO HIDE!
TONIGHT WE DINE ON PORK!
KEEP AWAY FROM THESE INNOCENTS, EXECUTIONER--
--YOUR HUNT IS RESTRICTED TO THE PIG AND THE PIG ALONE!
BWOM
GET PARKER TO THE DETENTION ROOM, NOW!
IS THIS "DETENTION ROOM" SAFE?
NO, BUT IT HAS A SECRET PASSAGEWAY TO SOMEWHERE THAT IS.
LET'S GO!

THE S.H.I.E.L.D. HELICARRIER.
MINUTES LATER.
RELAX--
--YOU'RE THREE THOUSAND FEET IN THE AIR NOW. YOU'LL BE FINE UNTIL THIS ALL BLOWS OVER.
THERE'S A "WHEN PIGS FLY" JOKE IN HERE SOMEWHERE, I KNOW IT.
GIMME A SEC, I'LL THINK OF IT!
DIRECTOR FURY, THERE ARE UNIDENTIFIED OBJECTS APPROACHING!
WHA--?
"HOW'S THAT POSSIBLE?"

THOSE WOLVES HAVE WINGS!
WHATEVER YOU DO, DON'T LET THEM IN!
I'VE GOT TO GET OUT THERE!
NO, YOU ARE STAYING HERE--
WE ARE GOING OUT THERE!
I CAN'T BELIEVE ALL OF THESE PEOPLE WOULD RISK THEIR LIVES JUST FOR LITTLE OLD ME.
LET THIS BE A LESSON TO YOU, SPIDER-HAM--
BE CAREFUL WHAT YOU WISH FOR.
YOU OFTEN COMPLAIN ABOUT NOT GETTING ANY RESPECT, AND NOW?
NOW YOU'RE LETTING OTHERS FIGHT YOUR BATTLES FOR YOU.
I QUESTION THE WISDOM OF TURNING YOU INTO A PIG.
PERHAPS A CHICKEN WOULD BE MORE APPROPRIATE.
THAT'S IT!

I AM SKURGE THE EXECUTIONER!
AND NOTHING STANDS BETWEEN ME AND MY PREY!
YOU SPEAK TOO SOON, EXECUTIONER!
SO SAYS THE PRINCE OF ASGARD!
AND THE PRINCIPAL OF MIDTOWN HIGH!
AIM FOR THEIR SOFT SPOTS.
LOKI! SHOW YOURSELF!
COME OUT AND FACE ME LIKE A MAN!
HUH?
NO! LEAVE MY FRIENDS OUT OF THIS!
THIS IS BETWEEN US!
YIELD, SKURGE!

NEVER!
UHN!
KLODD!
INCOMING PIG!
I'M TIRED OF LETTING MY FRIENDS PUT THEMSELVES IN HARM'S WAY FOR ME!
YOU WANT ME? HERE I AM!
CHOMP! CHOMP! CHOMP!

GET OFF OF ME!
THUNK!
I'VE NEVER SEEN A PIG DEFEND HIS HONOR SO GREATLY...
BUT IT'S TIME TO CHOP THE PORK!
BRRRROOOOOOOOOOOO
BRRRROOOOOOO

IT'S SUNDOWN!
THE HUNT IS OVER!
IT WAS A GLORIOUS HUNT, BUT TODAY THE BOAR HAS WON.
WHAT? THAT'S IT? IT'S OVER?
POOF!
NO!
THIS IS MADNESS!
YOU HAD HIM! STRIKE HIM DOWN!
WE HUNTERS LIVE BY A CODE OF HONOR.
THE HUNT IS OVER.
FINE! IF YOU WON'T FINISH THE JOB, THEN I WILL!

THAT'S WHAT YOU THINK!
POOF!
THE HUNT'S EXPIRED, AND SO HAS YOUR MAGIC SPELL!
THE PIG WAS A MORTAL?
AYE. MY BROTHER HAS ATTEMPTED TO TRICK YOU INTO DOING HIS EVIL DEEDS FOR HIM.
AND HIS PLAN MIGHT HAVE WORKED IF IT WASN'T FOR YOU, THOR.

AND THE REST OF YOU.
THANK YOU.

WE STILL NEED SOMETHING TO ROAST AT THE FEAST TONIGHT.
PERHAPS WE'LL HAVE SOME USE FOR LOKI AFTER ALL.
GOODBYE, SPIDER-MAN!
YOU WOULD HAVE MADE A SUCCULENT MEAL!
AW, SHUCKS.
WELL, AT LEAST ONE GOOD THING CAME OUT OF TODAY--
--AT LEAST I'LL GET ONE YEAR WITHOUT AN EMBARRASSING SCHOOL PICTURE.
GUESS AGAIN, WEB-HEAD!
OH NO!
HA! HA! HA! HA!
TH-TH-TH-THAT'S ALL FOLKS!

MARVEL UNIVERSE ULTIMATE SPIDER-MAN 30

Based on “I Am Spider-Man”

I'M PETER PARKER, AND I AM SPIDER-MAN!
I KNOW WHAT YOU'RE THINKING:
"DID SPIDER-MAN JUST GIVE OUT HIS SECRET IDENTITY?"
"HAS HE GONE COMPLETELY BONKERS?"
THE ANSWER IS YES. BUT ALLOW ME TO EXPLAIN. IT ALL STARTED A FEW WEEKS AGO AT MIDTOWN HIGH...
AHHHHH!
I CAN'T BELIEVE IT! I JUST CAN'T BELIEVE IT!
LADIES, PLEASE...
...THERE'S ENOUGH OF ME TO GO AROU--
OOOF!
IT'S AMAZING!
SPECTACULAR!
SENSATIONAL!
HUH?!
SCHOOL MUSICAL AUDITIONS
WILD WILD WEB
SING
ALL
ALL DANCING
A MUSICAL?!
WRITTEN BY MARY JANE WATSON?!
A PRINCIPAL COULSON PRODUCTION?!
"THIS CAN'T BE REAL!"

OH IT'S REAL, PARKER.
THE DRAMA TEACHER GOT THE MUMPS AND THEY NEEDED SOMEONE TO FILL IN.
I INTEND TO MAKE THIS THE BEST MUSICAL PRODUCTION SINCE... WHAT'S THE ONE WITH ALL THE CATS?
BUT WHY ME?
SURELY THERE MUST HAVE BEEN SOME OTHER CHOICES FOR SUBJECTS!
HULK SCHOOL MUSICAL
SORRY, BUT SOMEONE IN DRAMA CLASS CHOSE SPIDER-MAN.
WELL, TOO BAD! I WON'T DO IT!
ACTUALLY, YOU MAKE A GOOD POINT. THE RISK OF EXPOSING YOUR SECRET IDENTITY IS TOO HIGH. NOT TO MENTION...
...YOU'RE ALL WRONG FOR THE PART.
I'M WRONG FOR THE PART OF...ME?
NOT YOU--
SPIDER-MAN!
WHO IN THIS SCHOOL WOULD MAKE A BETTER SPIDER-MAN THAN ME?

NEXT!
NEXT!
NEXT!
NEXT!
SEE, SAM? THERE'S NO REPLACING YOURS TRULY. HE'LL NEVER FIND ANYONE.
I'M NOT SURE WHY ANYONE WOULD MAKE A SPIDER-MAN MUSICAL WHEN MY SUPER HERO PERSONA OF NOVA IS AVAILABLE.
I'M SPIDER-MAN, EVIL-DOER!
AND YOU JUST GOT BIT!
?
GREAT PERFORMANCE, PERFECT BUILD--
--THAT'S OUR SPIDER-MAN!
WHAT?!
BUT, WHO--?

I'M SPIDER-MAN!
YEAH!
"FLASH THOMPSON!"
HE'S BEEN BULLYING ME SINCE PRE-K!
YOU'RE JUST JEALOUS THAT HE LOOKS BETTER IN YOUR COSTUME THAN YOU DO.
MY COSTUME? YOU GAVE HIM MY REAL COSTUME?
RELAX! HE DOESN'T KNOW IT BELONGS TO YOU.
BUT GIVING IT TO HIM WAS WORTH IT JUST TO GET THIS SHOT. PRICELESS!
DON'T WORRY...
"...I'M SURE HE'LL RETURN IT AFTER AUDITIONS."
SPIDER-MAN, SPIDER-MAN, DOES WHATEVER--
SPIDER-MAN! SO COOL!
HEY, FLASH! WAIT UP!
SPIDER-MAN WAITS FOR NO ONE, DOOF.
WEREN'T YOU SUPPOSED TO TURN IN YOUR COSTUME?
WHAT'S IT TO YOU? IT'S THIS THING CALLED "METHOD ACTING." TO PLAY A GREAT SPIDER-MAN, I HAVE TO BE A GREAT SPIDER-MAN.
YOU SHOULD BE CAREFUL IN THAT. SOME SUPER-CRAZY MIGHT THINK YOU'RE THE REAL DEAL.
LET 'EM! THEN WE'LL SEE THEM GET BIT!
AGAIN WITH THAT CATCH-PHRASE?

I WILL SAVE YOU ALL, CRAWLING UP YOUR WALL!
AND SPINNING, SPINNING, SPINNING YOU A WEB THAT WILL NOT LET YOU FALL!
KLASH!
STOP! THIEF!
SPIDER-MAN!
SPIDER-MAN?! WHERE?!
I'LL SHOW YOU WHERE!
IT'S THE TRAPSTER! SPIDEY'S GLUE GUN-WIELDING NOT-SO-SUPER VILLAIN! WHAT DO I DO?
I HAVE NO COSTUME--
--IF I TRY ANYTHING, IT COULD GIVE AWAY MY SECRET IDENTITY!
SPLORCH!
WOW! LOOK AT THAT! YOUR SUPER SPIDEY REFLEXES HELPED YOU DODGE THAT FALLING STATUE!

THEY DID?
AT LEAST I STILL HAVE MY WEB-SHOOTERS.
BUT I CAN'T LET ANYONE SEE ME USING THEM.
I KNOW! NO ONE WOULD BE SUSPICIOUS IF ORDINARY TEENAGER PETER PARKER RAN AWAY FROM THE DANGEROUS SCENE--
--THEN NO ONE WILL NOTICE WHEN I SCALE THIS WALL TO THE ROOF FROM THE ALLEY!
PERFECT.
I'M SPIDER-MAN, EVIL-DOER!
THWAP
THWAP
LET'S HOPE MY PUPPETEERING SKILLS ARE UP TO SNUFF!

YOWWWWWW!
SPLORCH!
AND ONE MORE STRATEGICALLY PLACED WEB SHOT--
THWAP!
CRICK!
BINGO!
BOOONGG

HOW DID I GET OUT OF THE WAY OF THAT BLAST IN TIME?!
THIS METHOD ACTING REALLY WORKS.
HEY, YOU IN TV LAND! IF YOU WANT TO SEE MORE SPIDER-ACTION LIKE THIS, COME SEE MY SHOW AT MIDTOWN HIGH ON FRIDAY NIGHT!
FRIDAY, EH?
THEN THIS ISN'T OVER!
WHATEVER, LOSER!
I'M SPIDER-MAN, EVIL-DOER...
AND YOU JUST GOT BIT!
I LOVE THAT CATCH-PHRASE!
SPIDER-MAN EXCLUSIVE
BEE WITH 'LAKE CHARGOGGAGOGGMANCHAUGGAGOGGCHAUBUNAGUNGAMAUGG' - WORLD'S LARGEST ICE CREAM CONE MELTS. PANIC IN TH
FEEL FREE TO USE IT IN REAL BATTLE. MY GIFT TO YOU.
YOU CAN'T STILL BE CONSIDERING GOING THROUGH WITH THIS, CAN YOU?
IT'S TOO DANGEROUS!
I AGREE. THAT'S WHY I NAMED YOU AS FLASH'S UNDERSTUDY.
UNDERSTUDY?
UNDERSTUDY?!
DON'T WORRY, IT'S NOT LIKE YOU'LL ACTUALLY HAVE TO GO ON!
"PARKER, YOU'VE GOTTA GO ON!"

I CAN'T DO IT!
AS MUCH AS I'D LOVE TO WEAR THE COSTUME--WASH IT, THEN WEAR IT, RATHER--
--AS YOUR UNDERSTUDY, I'M HONOR-BOUND TO TELL YOU THAT IT'S PROBABLY JUST OPENING NIGHT JITTERS.
NO. I THOUGHT MY SINGING WOULD GE BETTER WITH PRACTICE, BUT I STINK!
SPIDER-MAN IS MY IDOL. I CAN'T MAKE HIM LOOK BAD BY HAVING EVERYONE LAUGH AT ME.
HE'S YOUR IDOL? REALLY?
THAT'S WEIRD.
WHAT'S SO WEIRD ABOUT THAT?
FOR ONE THING, HE USES HIS POWERS TO HELP PEOPLE. AND YOU USE YOURS TO...WELL...CRAM THEM INTO LOCKERS.
I WOULDN'T ABUSE REAL POWERS IF I HAD THEM.
BUT YOU DO HAVE THEM.
YOU'RE THE BIG MAN ON CAMPUS. A STAR ATHLETE.
PEOPLE WOULD IDOLIZE YOU THE WAY YOU IDOLIZE SPIDER-MAN IF YOU DIDN'T ACT LIKE SUCH A JERK.
YOU WANT TO BE LIKE YOUR HERO? THEN BE RESPONSIBLE FOR YOUR CHOICE.
GO OUT THERE AND FACE YOUR FEAR.
I-- I--
--I'M GONNA THROW UP!
BLERFT!
BLAAARRRGGHH!
IN THE BUCKET! IN THE BUCKET! NOT ON THE COSTUME!

I'M PRETTY SURE THAT PART OF AN UNDERSTUDY'S JOB ISN'T TO GET RID OF THE BARF BUCKETS.
HOPEFULLY NOW THAT FLASH GOT IT OUT OF HIS SYSTEM-- LITERALLY--HE'LL BE ABLE TO--
UH-OH!
IT'S THE TRAPSTER! HE ACTUALLY SHOWED!
AND HE'S STANDING RIGHT OUTSIDE OF FLASH'S DRESSING ROOM!
SURPRISE, WALL-CRAWLER!
HUH?!
KICK!
LIKE IT OR NOT, UNDERSTUDY, IT'S TIME TO HIT THE STAGE.
BUT FIRST--
--A WARDROBE CHANGE!

YOU MADE A BIG MISTAKE COMING HERE, TRAPSTER!
ANOTHER SPIDER-MAN?!

Midtown High Proudly Presents:
IT'S A WILD WILD WEB
GASP! WHO ARE YOU?
WE ARE THE FRIGHTFUL FOURRR!
IF ONLY THERE WERE SOMEONE WHO COULD SAVE US!
WE NEED A HERO!

KRASH!
LET'S TAKE THIS OUTSIDE WHERE NO ONE GETS HURT, TRAPSTER!
TRAPSTER?! NO! IT'S THE FRIGHTFUL FOU--!
OOPS, I MEAN..
DON'T YOU MEAN THE FRIGHTFUL FOUR?
I DIDN'T KNOW WE COULD IMPROV!
AFTER YOUR SHAMELESS PROMOTION ON THE NEWS, DON'T YOU THINK YOU OWE YOUR ADORING PUBLIC A REAL SHOW?
OU WANT ME TO GIVE THEM A SHOW?
YOU GOT IT!
HNN!
THAT'S NOT FLASH! THAT'S PETER!
IS THAT... THE REAL TRAPSTER?
WHAT ARE YOU DOING? STICK TO THE SCRIPT!
SECOND ACT FIGHT MUSIC. AND PLAY IT LOUD!

THE FIGHT SCENES ACTUALLY LOOK LIKE OUR REAL BATTLES AS S.H.I.E.L.D. AGENTS IN TRAINING, SAM.
YEAH. FLASH LOOKS JUST AS BAD OUT THERE AS PETER DOES IN REAL LIFE!
REAL? MORE LIKE REAL BORING!
AVA AYALA, A.K.A. WHITE TIGER.
SAM ALEXANDER, A.K.A. NOVA.
DANNY RAND, A.K.A. IRON FIST.
LUKE CAGE, A.K.A. POWER MAN.
SO...YOU'RE NOT EVEN THE REAL SPIDER-MAN?
DOESN'T MATTER. I'LL CRUSH YOU ANYWAY!
IS THAT RIGHT, PASTE POT PETE?
MY NAME'S THE TRAPSTER--
OOF!
SO FAKE! YOU CAN SEE THE ROPES AND EVERYTHING!
SORRY, MRS. PARKER!
SSSHH!
WOOO!
WAY TO GO, SPIDEY!
SPIDER-MAN RULES!

THEY LIKE ME! THEY REALLY LIKE ME!
LET'S SEE IF THEY LIKE THIS!
SPLORCH!
WHOA!
HNN...
FLASH, ARE YOU ALL RIGHT?
AUNT MAY? AUNT MAY, IS THAT YOU?
P-PETER?
LET'S GO, RED. YOU'RE COMING WITH ME!
THAT...DIDN'T LOOK SO FAKE TO ME.
HM.
SSSHHH!

I'M NOT GOING ANYWHERE WITH YOU!
YOU RUINED MY PLAY!
SOCKO!
HUH?
YOU HEARD THE LADY!
WHOOSH!
THE ONLY PLACE YOU'RE GOING...
...IS EXIT STAGE LEFT!
YAAAAAA!

HEY, TRAPSTER, YOU LEFT SOMETHING BEHIND.
SPLORCH!
THIS OUGHTTA GUM UP YOUR WORKS.
B-BEATEN... BY MY OWN WEAPONS.
AND BY A HIGH SCHOOL KID.
THE GUYS AT THE BAR WITH NO NAME WILL NEVER LET ME LIVE THIS DOWN.
AHEM
?
IT'S TIME FOR YOUR BIG MUSICAL NUMBER.
SPIDEY! SPIDEY!
SPIDEY!
WHAT?! NO WAY! I DON'T WANT ANY PART OF THIS!
SPIDEY! SPIDEY!
THEY THINK IT'S A SHOW. IT CAN'T END WITHOUT THE GRAND FINALE!

...
I WILL SAVE YOU ALL BY CRAWLING UP YOUR WALL...
...AND SPINNING, SPINNING, SPINNING YOU A WEB THAT WILL NOT LET YOU FALL.
I'M SPIDER-MAN! I'M SPIDER-MAN!
I AM SPIDER-MANNNNNN!
YOU DON'T HAVE TO ASK THE MAN BEHIND THIS MASK...
...WILL ANSWER, ANSWER EVERY CALL. I'M HERE TO SAVE YOU ALL!
THIS WILL BE WHAT THEY REMEMBER ME BY!
I'M SPIDER-MAN! I SPIDER-AM!
I AM SPIDER-MANNNNN!
AR

I AM SPIDER-MAN, EVIL-DOER! AND YOU JUST GOT BIT!
WOOO!
SPIDER-MAN RULES!
FLASH!
FLASH!
FLASH!
FLASH!
FLASH!
THEY THINK I'M FLASH?!
OH, COME ON!
FLASH! FLASH! FLASH! FLASH!
SHOW THEM WHO YOU REALLY ARE! YOU'RE JUST "ACTING," REMEMBER?
OH! RIGHT!
I'M PETER PARKER, AND I AM SPIDER-MAN!

YOU MEAN...
...IT WAS REAL?
PETER? THIS WHOLE TIME?
HEY, MJ, WHAT HAPPENED?
WHY DON'T YOU ASK YOUR UNDERSTUDY, AND THAT WEIRD CREEP HE LET INTO OUR HIGH SCHOOL MUSICAL?
BOOOOOOO!
WE WANT FLASH!
WE WANT FLASH!
WE WANT FLASH!
WE WANT FLASH!

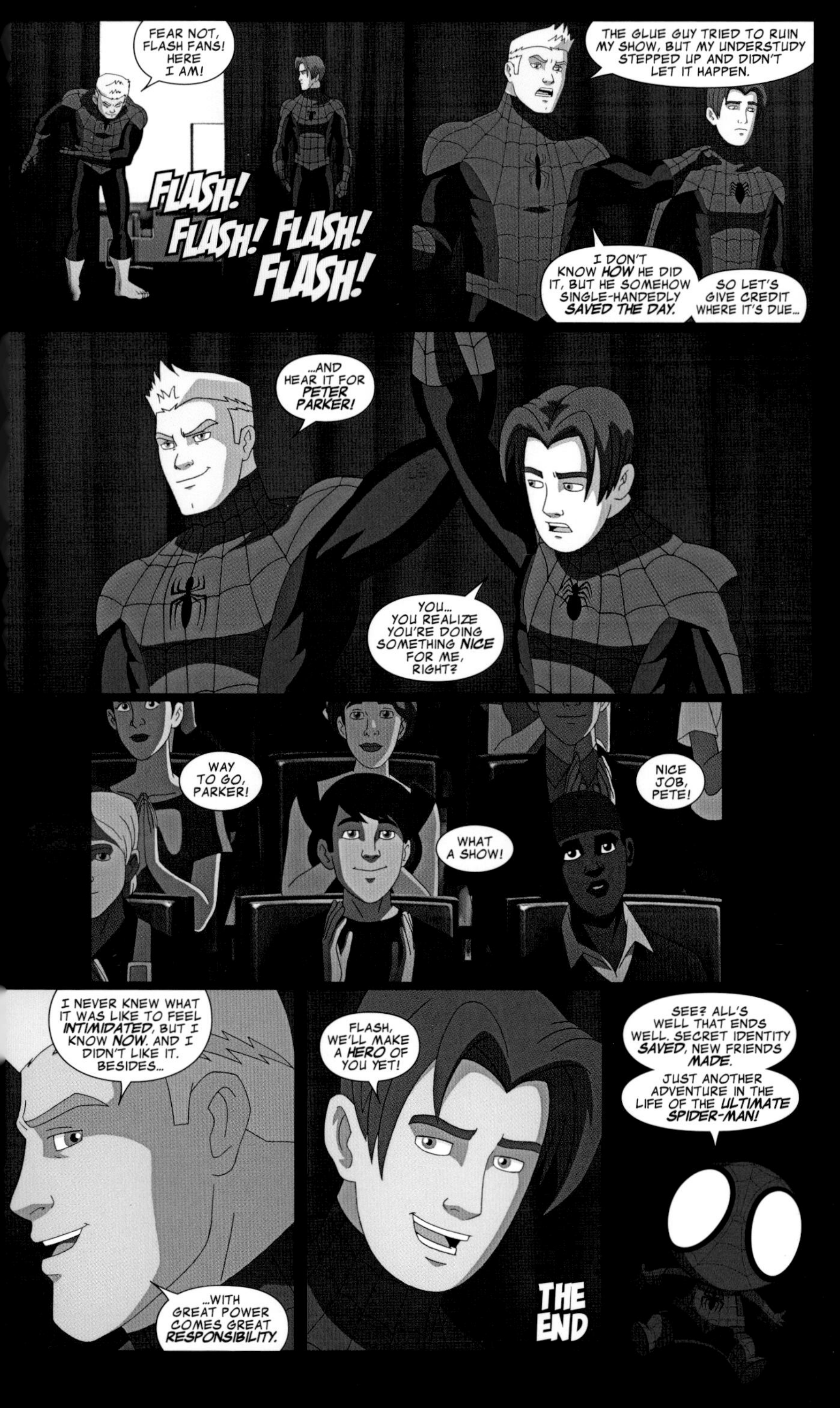
FEAR NOT, FLASH FANS! HERE I AM!
FLASH! FLASH! FLASH! FLASH!
THE GLUE GUY TRIED TO RUIN MY SHOW, BUT MY UNDERSTUDY STEPPED UP AND DIDN'T LET IT HAPPEN.
I DON'T KNOW HOW HE DID IT, BUT HE SOMEHOW SINGLE-HANDEDLY SAVED THE DAY.
SO LET'S GIVE CREDIT WHERE IT'S DUE...
...AND HEAR IT FOR PETER PARKER!
YOU... YOU REALIZE YOU'RE DOING SOMETHING NICE FOR ME, RIGHT?
WAY TO GO, PARKER!
WHAT A SHOW!
NICE JOB, PETE!
I NEVER KNEW WHAT IT WAS LIKE TO FEEL INTIMIDATED, BUT I KNOW NOW. AND I DIDN'T LIKE IT. BESIDES...
...WITH GREAT POWER COMES GREAT RESPONSIBILITY.
FLASH, WE'LL MAKE A HERO OF YOU YET!
SEE? ALL'S WELL THAT ENDS WELL. SECRET IDENTITY SAVED, NEW FRIENDS MADE.
JUST ANOTHER ADVENTURE IN THE LIFE OF THE ULTIMATE SPIDER-MAN!
THE END

Based on "The Iron Octopus"

LINE UP YOUR LAWYERS, STARK--
--YOUR SO-CALLED "TECH" NEARLY DESTROYED ME! AND MY SON HARRY!
HAVEN'T YOU BEEN LISTENING?
"YES, IT WAS MY TECH THAT BROKE INTO YOUR OFFICE AT OSCORP, NORMAN, BUT I DIDN'T DO IT!
"MY TECH ALSO ATTACKED ME AT STARK INDUSTRIES!
"SOMEONE--ERR, SOMETHING--HACKED MY MAINFRAME FIREWALLS AND STOLE VERY VALUABLE TECHNICAL DATA--INCLUDING MY ARMORS' REMOTE OPERATION CODES.
"IT LOOKED LIKE SOME KIND OF A MECHANIZED SPIDER."
I TOLD YOU I'D PAY FOR ALL OF THE DAMAGE. I EVEN CHOKED DOWN THE BILE AND APOLOGIZED--
IF THAT'S NOT GOOD ENOUGH FOR YOU, YOU CAN GO--
STOP!
YOU'RE BOTH GROWN-UPS! SO ACT LIKE IT!
AND BEFORE WE GO BLAMING SPIDERS, LET'S REMEMBER THERE ARE OTHER ANIMALS THAT HAVE EIGHT LEGS, TOO...
LIKE AN OCTOPUS.

DOCTOR CONNORS? WHAT'S UP?
THERE'S SOMETHING I NEED TO SHOW YOU. ALL OF YOU.
SOME MONTHS AGO, YOU BROUGHT ME A SAMPLE FROM THE UNDERWATER LAIR OF DOCTOR OCTOPUS. THIS NEW SPECIMEN IS A PERFECT MATCH.
AFTER FOLLOWING UP WITH EVERY RENOWNED ROBOTICS SCIENTIST IN THE WORLD, I FINALLY HAVE A TECHNOLOGICAL I.D.--
OTTO OCTAVIUS
--AN OLD FRIEND NAMED OTTO OCTAVIUS.
WE DID OUR GRADUATE STUDIES TOGETHER.
HE WAS BRILLIANT. DRIVEN.
AFTER GRADUATION HE FOUND A JOB WITH A MAJOR TECH COMPANY--
--OSCORP.
WHAT?! DOC OCK WORKED FOR YOU, MR. OSBORN?
I'VE NEVER HEARD OF A "DOC OCK"...
...BUT OTTO OCTAVIUS WAS LIKE ANOTHER SON TO ME...

WE WERE DOING REVOLUTIONARY WORK IN MY LAB, BUT THERE WAS A TERRIBLE ACCIDENT.
"OTTO PERISHED IN MY ARMS.
"THE NOTION THAT HE'S STILL ALIVE IS UTTERLY PREPOSTEROUS."
YET HERE'S OTTO'S WORK. OR SHOULD I SAY... OSCORP'S?
WHAT? NO! MY FATHER'S THE VICTIM HERE!
HARRY'S GOT A POINT-- INNOCENT UNTIL PROVEN GUILTY. THERE HAS TO BE SOME EXPLANATION FOR ALL OF THIS.
SPLASH
HUH? TELL ME I'M NOT THE ONLY ONE WHO SAW THE SEVERED TENTACLE MOVE.
KRIKK!
KRASH!
AAAAAH!

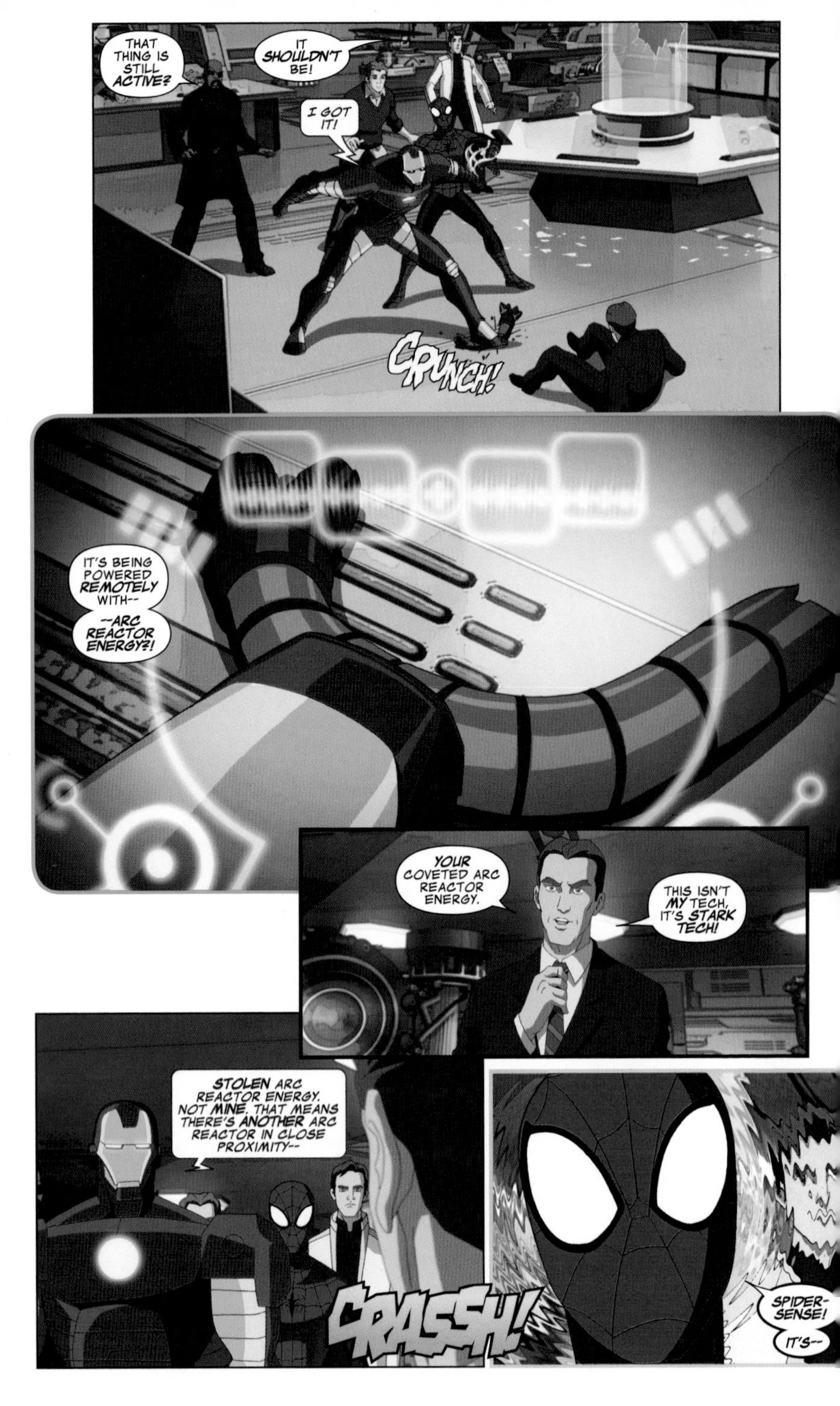
THAT THING IS STILL ACTIVE?
IT SHOULDN'T BE!
I GOT IT!
CRUNCH!
IT'S BEING POWERED REMOTELY WITH--
--ARC REACTOR ENERGY?!
YOUR COVETED ARC REACTOR ENERGY.
THIS ISN'T MY TECH, IT'S STARK TECH!
STOLEN ARC REACTOR ENERGY. NOT MINE. THAT MEANS THERE'S ANOTHER ARC REACTOR IN CLOSE PROXIMITY--
CRASSH!
SPIDER-SENSE!
IT'S--

-DOCTOR OCTOPUS!
IN A CUSTOMIZED SUIT OF ARMOR--COMPLETE WITH ARC REACTOR!
OKAY, EVERYONE WITHOUT AN OSTENTATIOUS SUPER-SUIT--TAKE COVER!

YOU SHOULDN'T PLAY WITH OTHER PEOPLES' TOYS WITHOUT PERMISSION, DOC!
IRON MAN, WAIT!
THWAK!
I ALREADY HAVE WHAT I NEED FROM YOU, TONY STARK!
UHN!
MY OCTOBOTS--
SHUNK!
SHUNK!
SMASH!
CLIK!
CLAK!
--TAKE THIS PRIMITIVE PREDECESSOR TO MY OCTO-ARMOR--
FSSSH!
"--FOR A JOYRIDE!"
JUST A HEADS UP, J.A.R.V.I.S.-- I MIGHT BE LATE FOR DINNER!
FROOOSH!

CALLING ALL AGENTS, THIS IS DIRECTOR FURY-- THERE'S AN INTRUDER IN THE LAB...AND HE'S ARMED!
EIGHT-ARMED, IN FACT!
SAVE THE JOKES FOR LATER, SPIDER-MAN--
--LIKE AFTER I BLAST HIS ARMOR INTO SCRAP METAL!
ZARK! ZARK! ZARK! ZARK!
DO YOU TRULY BELIEVE THAT I AM UNABLE TO ANSWER YOUR FIRE--
ZARK! ZARK!
BRAKKA! BRAKKA! BRAKKA! BRAKKA! BRAKKA!
--WITH SOME OF MY OWN?!
YOU ALL STAY HERE--LET THE PROS HANDLE THIS!
I DIG THE NEW DUDS, OCK! BUT SOMETHING'S MISSING.
YOU'RE IN LUCK, WE'RE RUNNING A SPECIAL ON SUPER VILLAIN ARMOR ACCESSORIES!
HERE, TRY ONE ON!

WAP!
ARGH!
GET OVER HERE, YOU INSOLENT PEST!
IT'S NORMAN OSBORN I WANT, BUT IF I HAVE TO DESTROY EACH AND EVERY ONE OF YOU TO GET TO HIM...
...THEN SO BE IT!
HMMM. SO MUCH FOR THE "PROS."

ZARK! ZARK! ZARK! ZARK!
EVERY TIME I BLAST ONE OF THESE OCTOBOTS TO BITS, ANOTHER TAKES ITS PLACE!
OSBORN!
THAT "ACCIDENT" IN YOUR LAB TOOK FROM ME EVERYTHING THAT WAS IMPORTANT.
SO I'M GOING TO DO THE SAME TO YOU!
D-DAD!
HARRY, I--
N-NO--
ARGH!
HARRY!
ZZSSSKKK!

RETRIBUTION IS AT HAND--
--BUT NOT HERE!
BR-KOOM!
YOU'RE BOTH COMING WITH ME!
NO!
THWAP! THWAP!
I CAN'T LET YOU TAKE THEM!
CAN'T... LET...
CRUD.
SLICE!

INTEL, TRACK THE BOGEY LEAVING THE HELICARRIER!
WE CAN'T LOSE HIM!
IT'S GOING TO TAKE EVERY AGENT WE'VE GOT TO CAPTURE OCK.
MAYBE NOT, FURY...
OTTO OCTAVIUS ISN'T THE ONLY ONE WITH FANCY ARMOR.
NEW YORK CITY.
BEG ME, OSBORN!
OSCORP

BEG ME TO SHOW YOUR SON THE MERCY YOU DIDN'T SHOW ME!
THIS HAS NOTHING TO DO WITH HARRY, OTTO!
IT DOES NOW!
OTTO...I'M YOUR FRIEND! AFTER THE ACCIDENT, I SAVED YOUR LIFE. THOSE WERE MY MACHINES THAT--
--THAT ENSLAVED ME!
YOU MADE ME A MONSTER!
ZZK
I'M HERE TO RETURN THE FAVOR!
THWAP!
HANDS OFF THE OSBORNS!
THWAP!
TINK!

WHAT, YOU THOUGHT YOU WERE THE ONLY ONE WITH A NEW LOOK?
GOODBYE, FRIENDLY NEIGHBORHOOD ULTIMATE SPIDER-MAN--
--HELLO, IRON SPIDER!
KA-RANG!
THIS IRON SPIDER ARMOR IS...
...WICKEDY-AWE-TASTIC!
MY ARMOR'S PRETTY COOL, HUH? SO COOL THAT THEY HAVEN'T YET INVENTED A WORD FOR HOW COOL IT IS.
SO I'LL DO IT NOW.

I'LL SEE YOU STRUNG UP BY YOUR WEBS FOR THAT!
BRAKKA! BRAKKA! BRAKKA! BRAKKA!
JUST FOR THAT? THERE ARE A LOT WORSE THINGS I'VE DONE TO BE STRUNG UP FOR.
FINE, PLAY THE FOOL. LIKE YOU'VE BEEN PLAYING ALL ALONG...WITH OSBORN.
HUH?
DON'T LISTEN TO HIM, SPIDER-MAN!
HE'S A LUNATIC!
I WORKED FOR OSBORN! WE STALKED YOU TOGETHER!
STUDYING YOU... TO STEAL YOUR SECRETS!
RIIIGGGHHHHT... BECAUSE INSANE DUDES IN IRON OCTOPUS ARMOR ARE ALWAYS THE ONES YOU CAN COUNT ON TO TELL THE TRUTH.

WE DID IT ALL! THE ATTACKS! THE LIES!
ALL OF THE PROBLEMS IN YOUR LIFE THESE PAST FEW MONTHS ARE THE FAULT OF ONE MAN--
--NORMAN OSBORN!
THP! THP! THP! THP! THP! THP!
YOU'RE LYING!
AAAAAH!
TAK! TAK! TAK! TAK! TAK! TAK! TAK!
HHHRRRNNN...
HE MANAGED TO GRAB ON AFTER HE FELL OVER THE LEDGE...
HUFF HUFF HUFF
...BUT NOW'S YOUR CHANCE, MR. OSBORN! GET HARRY TO SAFETY!
THANKS, SPIDER-MAN.
WAIT! WHAT DOC OCK SAID ABOUT YOU AND HIM--IS ANY OF THAT TRUE?

OTTO OCTAVIUS IS PSYCHOTIC AND DELUSIONAL.
YOU HAVE DONE MORE FOR MY FAMILY THAN I CAN EVER THANK YOU FOR.
YOU CAN TRUST ME.
WE TRUST HIM...DON'T WE?
HA! WE DON'T EVEN TRUST YOU!
YOINK!
SNAG!
USE YOUR BRAIN, SPIDER-MAN! EVERY WORD THAT MAN UTTERS IS A LIE--
I'M DONE LISTENING TO YOU, OCTAVIUS!
ZZAAAKKK!
ARGH!
M-MY ARC REACTOR!
SKRRSH!

WHAT DID YOU DO TO MY ARC REACTOR? WHAT'S WRONG WITH IT?
I HAVE THE SAME PROBLEM WITH MY CELL PHONE.
DID YOU REMEMBER TO CHARGE IT?
CRACK!
HEY! THAT HURT!
I'VE HAD ENOUGH OF YOUR JOKES!
KROOM!
I PROMISE, THIS WON'T HURT... FOR LONG.
LET HIM GO!
WH-WHO--
ZARK!
ZARK! ZARK! ZARK! ZARK! ZARK!
TOOK YOU LONG ENOUGH!
SORRY. IT ISN'T EVERY DAY I GET ROCKETED TO THE THERMOSPHERE BY SQUID BOTS.

WHY ISN'T THE ARC REACTOR REPOWERING? IT SHOULD BE SELF-SUSTAINING!
I BUILT IT TO YOUR EXACT SPECIFICATIONS!
OFF THE SPECS YOU STOLE. BUT I NEVER PUT EVERYTHING IN A COMPUTER.
ALL THE GOOD STUFF'S UP HERE.
EXCEPT FOR THE ARMORS' REMOTE OPERATION CODES, APPARENTLY.
TOO SOON.
I WILL NOT LET IT END THIS WAY!
WILL YOU DO THE HONORS, KID?
IT'LL BE MY PLEASURE!
VMM!
I DID THAT?!
WITH THE ARMOR I BUILT.
WHICH I UPGRADED.
USING MY TECHNOLOGY.

LATER...
MY AGENTS HAVE SEARCHED THE WHOLE CITY, BUT THERE'S NO TRACE OF OCK ANYWHERE.
HE HAD TO HAVE LANDED SOMEWHERE.
IF IT'LL MAKE YOU FEEL BETTER, I CAN PROVIDE AROUND-THE-CLOCK SECURITY TO ENSURE YOUR SAFETY--
THAT WON'T BE NECESSARY, FURY. I HAVE MY OWN DETAIL.
THANK YOU, SPIDER-MAN. FOR EVERYTHING. YOU SAVED ME. AGAIN.
NO SWEAT. IT'S WHAT WE DO, HARRY.
I WANT YOU TO KNOW, MR. OSBORN, I'LL BE KEEPING AN EYE ON YOU...
...JUST IN CASE ANY MORE EX-EMPLOYEES SHOW UP WITH ACCUSATIONS.
OCK IS A MADMAN, BUT EVEN A BROKEN CLOCK IS RIGHT TWICE A DAY.
"IT'S MESSING WITH MY HEAD, YOU KNOW?"

EVEN LATER...
I WANT TO GIVE NORMAN THE BENEFIT OF THE DOUBT FOR HARRY'S SAKE--
--MAYBE FOR MINE TOO--
--BUT THE THINGS THAT OCK SAID--
I'M SO CONFUSED!
WE ALL HAVE PEOPLE WE LOOK UP TO, SPIDER-MAN, BUT SOMETIMES THEY AREN'T WHO WE THINK THEY ARE.
USE YOUR HEAD. LISTEN TO YOUR GUT. FOLLOW YOUR HEART.
AND IF YOU NEED SOMEONE TO LOOK UP TO, WELL, THERE'S ALWAYS ME.
SO...
DO WE HUG NOW?
YOU DO, AND I'LL UNIBEAM YOU TO DETROIT.
SEE YOU AROUND, KID!
YOU WILL?
DOES THAT MEAN MORE TEAM-UPS?
IF YOU'RE LUCKY.
THE END

Based on "In Deep"

ARE YOU SURE THIS IS THE LOCATION?
WHEN AM I EVER WRONG?
DON'T BE SO JUMPY, "CROSSBONES."
JUMPY, "GRIM REAPER"? HYDRA IS MY SPECIALTY, REMEMBER? IT'S NOT ME THAT I'M WORRIED ABOUT.
WHAT'S THAT SUPPOSED TO MEAN?
JUST STICK TO THE PLAN. KEEP SURPRISES TO A MINIMUM.
SURPRISES? MOI?
KNOCK, KNOCK.
VRRT!
COME IN.
DO YOU HAVE WHAT YOU PROMISED ME?
SURE DO.
DOES THAT MEAN WE'RE ALLOWED INTO YOUR SUPER VILLAIN CLUB...
...RED SKULL?
SPLENDID.
LAUNCH THE SUB.

"SUB"? THIS THING'S A SUBMARINE?
OKAY, SO I DON'T KNOW EVERYTHING.
FWOOSH!
M.O.D.O.K., THEY'VE ARRIVED.
SHOULD WE DESTROY THEM FOR WASTING OUR TIME?
HMM.
VMMMM!
AH! WHERE'D HE COME FROM?
NO. THEY'RE TELLING THE TRUTH. THIS IS DEFINITELY STARK'S ARMOR.
BUT HE'S EMBEDDED IT WITH NEURO-INHIBITORS TO PROTECT HIMSELF FROM MY TECHNO-PATHIC ABILITIES.
WERE YOU AWARE OF THIS?
WHAT DO I KNOW? I'M JUST THE GRIM REAPER, REMEMBER?
BAH!
MEN, BRING THIS IRON CARCASS TO MY LAB. THERE'S MORE THAN ONE WAY TO CRACK HIM!
AND WHILE YOU'RE DOING THAT...

"...I'LL SHOW OUR VISITORS AROUND."
IT IS SAID THAT TOGETHER THE AVENGERS FACE THREATS NO SINGLE HERO CAN.
IT IS ONLY FITTING THAT WE, THEIR GREATEST FOES, ALL WORK TOGETHER...
BDEET!
...IN ORDER TO DESTROY THEM!
BREATHTAKING, IS IT NOT? WE'RE BUILDING AN ARMY UNLIKE THE WORLD HAS EVER SEEN.
WOW.
HOW MANY TROOPS DO YOU HAVE?
MORE IMPORTANTLY, WHAT ARE YOU PAYING THEM?
WHAT'S YOUR NEXT TARGET?
WHAT KIND OF POWER SOURCE DOES THIS SUB USE?
DEET DEET DEET DEET
SO MANY QUESTIONS...
...BUT I SEE THAT OUR OTHER GUEST HAS FINALLY ARRIVED.

OTHER GUEST?
WE'VE GOT TO BE TWO THOUSAND FEET DEEP BY NOW--

"--WHO COULD POSSIBLY BE KNOCKING ON THE DOOR?"

NOW LET US SEE IF YOU CAN DO AS YOU CLAIM.
COME, WARLORD. YOU WILL SEE THAT EVERYTHING WE AGREED TO IS GOING AS PLANNED.
KEEP AN EYE ON HIS SOLDIERS.
IF THE WEAPON HE PROVIDED US DOES AS HE SAYS...
...OUR WAR WITH THE AVENGERS ENDS TODAY!
AVENGERS TOWER. NEW YORK CITY.
I KNEW THIS PLAN WAS A LOAD OF HOOEY--

--IF SKULL PUT THE KNUCKLE DOWN ON OUR MEN, WE'VE GOT TROUBLE WITH A CAPITAL "T."
THAT'S THE WORST CAP IMPRESSION EVER...
...HAWKEYE.
WHAT?
THAT'S TOTALLY THE OLD-TIMEY WAY THAT CAP TALKS, WIDOW.
WHAT'S THE SIGNAL ON THEIR LOCATION THERE, FALCON, OLD CHUM?
UM, RIGHT.
ACTUALLY, THEIR SIGNAL WENT ON THE MOVE. I CAN'T FIND IT ANYWHERE.
LET'S HOPE THEY CAN CALL IT IN.
THAT'S WHAT YOU GET WHEN YOU SEND STEVE ROGERS AND TONY STARK ON A SPY MISSION.
YOU SHOULD'VE SENT ME. THAT'S MY SPECIALTY, REMEMBER?
YEAH, BUT REAPER'S AND CROSSBONES' COSTUMES DIDN'T FIT YOU.
I'M GONNA HOOK UP WITH S.H.I.E.L.D. TO TRY AND TRACK THEM ANOTHER WAY--
"--LET'S HOPE THIS DOESN'T MEAN THEIR COVER'S BEEN BLOWN!"
THERE'S NO TECHNOLOGY YOU CAN BUILD THAT I CAN NOT UNDO, STARK.

I'M COMING FOR YOU, STARK.
WHRRRRRRRR
A-HA! I KNEW YOU COULDN'T KEEP ME OUT!
CH-CHAK!
WHAT?! IT'S EMPTY!
WE'VE BEEN TRICKED!
SECURITY BREACH!
REAPER AND CROSSBONES ARE NOT WHO THEY SAY THEY ARE! BRING THEM TO MY LAB IMMEDIATELY!
UH-OH.
HEY, HOW DO YOU KNOW STARK DIDN'T TRICK US TOO?
FACE IT, PARTNER...

...THE JIG IS UP!
BUT THESE GUYS ARE GOING DOWN!
WHOOSH
DO MY EARS DECEIVE ME? DID STEVE ROGERS JUST MAKE A JOKE?
I'M GOOD FOR A CHUCKLE EVERY NOW AND AGAIN.
SURE, YOU'RE A LAUGH A MINUTE.
BUT THIS IS NO JOKE. MY AVENGERS I.D. CARD ISN'T WORKING. I CAN'T CALL FOR BACKUP.
M.O.D.O.K. MUST HAVE TECH DAMPENERS ABOARD THIS THING.
SO? WE CAN STILL HANDLE OURSELVES.
AHH!
BUT WITHOUT TECH YOU'RE STILL ALL CAPTAIN AMERICA-LIKE, STEVE. WITHOUT MY IRON MAN ARMOR, I'M JUST A REGULAR PERSON.
ONLY WITH A SWISS BANK ACCOUNT AND GREAT HAIR.
THEN WE HAVE NO CHOICE. ABORT THE MISSION JUST AS WE PLANNED.
CRACK!
BUT WE DIDN'T PLAN ON BEING IN A SUBMARINE SURROUNDED BY ATLANTEAN SOLDIERS.
TAKKA TAKKA TAKKA TAKKA
MAYBE I CAN HACK INTO M.O.D.O.K.'S COMPUTERS, FIND HIS LAB, TURN OFF HIS DAMPENERS AND TAKE MY ARMOR BACK.

EXCEPT M.O.D.O.K.'S GOON SQUAD IS CLOSING IN ON US!
ABORT, TONY! THERE'S NO TIME!
"THERE'S ALWAYS TIME WHEN YOU'RE TONY STARK!"
WHERE DID THEY GO?!
PATHETIC.
DON'T JUST LIE THERE, ATLANTEANS! CHECK OUTSIDE THE SHIP!
WATCH IT, SKULL! MY WARRIORS ONLY TAKE ORDERS FROM ME.
THEN YOU TELL YOUR INCOMPETENT HORDES TO DO AS I SAY.
INCOMPETENT? LIKE YOUR MEN WHO LET THE AVENGERS ON BOARD IN THE FIRST PLACE?
WARRIORS! LET US SHOW HERR SKULL WHAT WE ARE CAPABLE OF. BRING THE AVENGERS TO ME!

I KNEW THAT LETTING ATTUMA JOIN OUR CABAL WOULD BE A MISTAKE.
YOU'RE ONE TO TALK. WHAT KIND OF A TECHNOPATH CAN'T FIND TWO HUMANS ON A SUBMARINE?
WE DON'T EVEN KNOW THAT THEY'RE STILL ON BOARD, SKULL!
IF THEY ARE OUT IN THE OCEAN, NOW IS AS GOOD A TIME AS ANY TO SHOW YOU WHAT THE WEAPON I BROUGHT CAN DO.
BRING ME THE TRIDENT!
SO THE CABAL AIN'T THE WELL-OILED MACHINE SKULL MADE IT OUT TO BE.
LISTEN TO THEM BICKER! LIKE KIDS IN A TREE HOUSE!
SOUNDS FAMILIAR.
WAIT-- WHAT ARE YOU SAYING?
WE HAD ESCAPE PROTOCOLS. YOU WENT OFF-PLAN.
YOU'RE LUCKY I GOT US INTO THIS AIR SHAFT IN TIME.
YOU'RE, WHAT, THE THIRD SMARTEST PERSON IN THE WORLD? YOU SHOULD KNOW THAT WE HATCHED THESE PLANS FOR A REASON.
IT'S ALMOST LIKE YOU DON'T WANT US TO GET OUT OF HERE IN ONE PIECE!
ARE YOU SUGGESTING...
...THAT THERE ARE TWO PEOPLE WHO ARE SMARTER THAN ME?

YES! THE TRIDENT OF NEPTUNE!
THE POWER OF THE OCEAN ITSELF!
WITH ITS POWER AT OUR DISPOSAL, EARTH'S MIGHTIEST HEROES SHALL FALL, AND ALL THE NATIONS OF THE WORLD WILL FOLLOW!
YOU WANT A PLAN? I'VE GOT A PLAN.
OH REALLY? WHAT IS IT?
TO GET CAUGHT.
HEY, ANYONE KNOW WHERE I CAN GET A GIANT, GOLDEN SALAD FORK AROUND HERE?
TONY, WHAT ARE YOU DOING?
TONY STARK?! YOU SURRENDER?

WHAT ELSE COULD I DO? I WAS NEVER MUCH OF A SWIMMER, TO BE HONEST.
DO YOU EVEN KNOW WHAT A PLAN IS?
I'M NOT SEEING THE BRILLIANCE OF THIS.
YOU'RE JUST NOT LOOKING CLOSE ENOUGH, STEVE.
NOW TO SEE IF THE TRIDENT OF NEPTUNE LIVES UP TO ITS LEGEND.

WHAT ARE YOU DOING? YOU'LL RUPTURE THE HULL!
CRACK!
FLOOSH!
HA HA HA HA HA
WHOOSH!
WHOA!
SPLASH!
IT'S TRUE! THE POWER TO COMMAND THE SEA!
I HAVE JUST WEAPONIZED WATER! THREE QUARTERS OF THE EARTH IS MINE TO CONTROL!

"YOU"? DON'T YOU MEAN "WE"?!
OR HAVE YOU BEEN PLANNING TO KEEP IT FOR YOURSELF ALL ALONG?
ONLY ONE CAN WIELD IT AT A TIME, M.O.D.O.K.
EH?
THAT WAS NOT OUR AGREEMENT--
--I AM THE RIGHTFUL LORD OF ANYTHING WHOSE POWER DERIVES FROM THE OCEAN.
NO! I CAPTURED STEVE ROGERS AND TONY STARK! IT IS MY RIGHT TO DESTROY THEM!
IS THIS FOR REAL?
SSHHH!
YOU DARE?! I AM A KING! YOU ARE NOTHING BUT THE RED SKULL'S LAPDOG!
YOU'RE NOTHING BUT A FISHMONGER! I AM M.O.D.O.K.!

ENOUGH!
DON'T YOU SEE THEY SEEK TO DIVIDE US? FOOLS!
I HAVE HAD ENOUGH OF YOUR INSULTS, SKULL! YOU ONLY SEEK TO POSSESS THE TRIDENT ON YOUR OWN!
HEY, M.O.D.O.K.--
--YOU'VE GOT SOMETHING ON YOUR FOREHEAD!
WHOOSH!
CLANG!
FZZZT!
WH-WHAT... HAVE YOU DONE...?

ACCORDING TO MY ARMOR'S TRACKING DEVICE, HE JUST SHUT DOWN YOUR TECH DAMPENERS!
ARE YOU SURE?
I'LL KNOW FOR SURE IN ABOUT TEN SECONDS IF MY ARMOR GETS HERE!
KRZZZT!
TEN SECONDS?
I CAN BUY US TEN SECONDS!
WHUDD!
AND HERE IT IS!
COME TO DADDY, SWEE' PEA!
CHK!
GOODBYE, TONY STARK, ORDINARY GUY--
CHAK!

HELLO, IRON MAN!
OOF!
KLAK!
YOU'RE TOO LATE TO STOP ME, IRON MAN!
NOT EVEN YOUR ARMOR CAN SAVE YOU FROM--
SPLURRSHH!
--THIS!
HNN!
TONY!

YOU THINK TOO SMALL, SKULL--
POW!
ATTUMA SHALL SHOW YOU THE TRUE POWER OF THE SEVEN SEAS!
FLRRSSHH!

AS MUCH AS I LOVE TO WATCH YOU SQUABBLE--
--THIS KIND OF POWER IS TOO DANGEROUS TO LEAVE IN ANYONE'S HANDS!
I'M PUTTING AN END TO IT NOW!
NO! ROGERS, DO YOU REALIZE WHAT YOU'VE DONE?
YOU'VE UNLEASHED THE FULL POWER OF NEPTUNE!
"YOU HAVE ANGERED THE OCEAN ITSELF!"

NO!
AAAAH!
AND WHAT DO YOU CALL THAT PLAN? "READY, SHOOT, AIM"?
I LEARNED FROM THE BEST.
NOW GET US OUT OF HERE!
ONE EMERGENCY EXIT COMING UP!
SPLOOSH!
HOLD YOUR BREATH!
THE FORCE OF THE WHIRLPOOL IS TOO STRONG FOR MY ARMOR!
WE'RE OUT OF THE WATER...
...BUT IT'S NOT ENOUGH! I'M SORRY--
--WE'RE FALLING BACK IN!
THAT'S OKAY! WHEN OUR TECH WENT BACK ONLINE... I CALLED THEM!

VOOOOOOSH!
THOR! I NEVER THOUGHT I'D BE SO HAPPY TO SEE YOU!
DO NOT MAKE ME REGRET SAVING YOU, STARK.
THANKS FOR THE PICKUP, WIDOW.
IT'S GOOD TO SEE THAT YOU BOYS MADE IT OUT OKAY. AND ARE PLAYING NICE.
LET'S JUST SAY THAT WE SAW WHAT IT LOOKS LIKE WHEN TEAMMATES DON'T GET ALONG, AND IT AIN'T PRETTY.
BUT I ALSO LEARNED HOW TO SEE THINGS CAP'S WAY. TURNS OUT THAT PLANNING CAN BE A GOOD THING. GO FIGURE.
THAT'S FUNNY, I LEARNED THAT SOMETIMES YOU HAVE TO GO OFF-PLAN TO GET THE JOB DONE.
AND I LEARNED THAT YOU TWO ARE EVEN MORE NAUSEATING WHEN YOU'RE GETTING ALONG.
THE END